Sarah Garland is a much-loved author/illustrator who has published more than 40 books for children. She has also written books for adults on herbs and wild plants, and their uses. The daughter of a publisher and illustrator, Sarah trained as a typographer at the London College of Printing.

She has four children and four grandchildren and lives near Cirencester, Gloucestershire. Her other books for Frances Lincoln include *Eddie's Garden, Eddie's Kitchen* and *Billy and Belle.*

For Tim and the children at Spinney Hill School

First published in Great Britain in 1994 by
The Bodley Head Children's Books

This edition published in 2009 by
Frances Lincoln Children's Books,
4 Torriano Mews, Torriano Avenue, London NW5 2RZ
www.franceslincoln.com

British Library Cataloguing in Publication Data
available on request

ISBN 978-1-84780-028-2

Illustrated with pen and watercolour
Set in Baskerville

Printed in Singapore

1 2 3 4 5 6 7 8 9

PASS IT, POLLY

Sarah Garland

F
FRANCES LINCOLN
CHILDREN'S BOOKS

Polly's school is Belmont Primary.
Polly's teacher is Mr Budd.

On Monday Mr Budd said:

Polly and Nisha were the only girls who put their hands up.

After lunch they got ready for their first practice game.

It will be so muddy!
Play rounders with us.
We can do it Polly!
Of course we can!

But the practice game did not go well.

It went very badly.

Polly and Nisha were muddy and cross.

They decided to look for a football book in the library.

They learnt some interesting things about fairies, fishes, fossils and Finland, but nothing very helpful about football.

They had tea at Polly's house.

I just can't understand how they do it.
Perhaps we will be better tomorrow.

But the next day was not much better

and they went back to Nisha's house after school feeling quite fed up.

Oh yes, I played football all right. Here I am in the army football team during the war.
Can you still remember how to play?
Please teach us, Grandpa.

Grandpa could remember and, after tea, he began to teach them all he knew.

On Tuesday he taught them how to pass the ball and how to stop it.

On Wednesday he taught them how to head the ball and how to dribble.

On Thursday he taught them how to trap the ball and how to throw it in.

And on Friday he taught them how to score a goal.

On Saturday the coach from Greenhill School arrived.

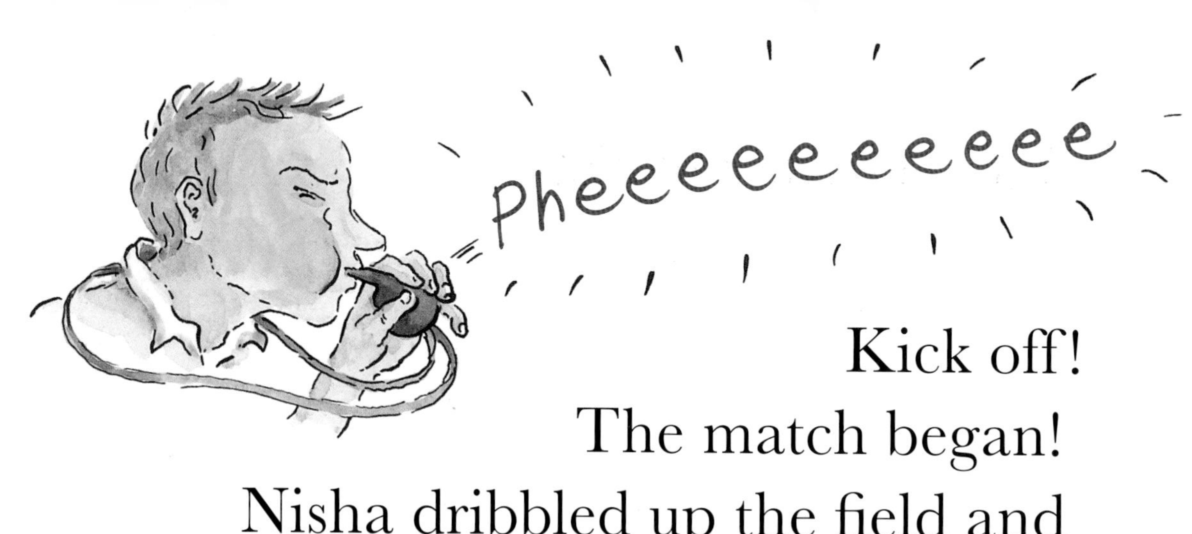

Kick off!
The match began!
Nisha dribbled up the field and
passed to Kiran.

Kiran passed to Polly.

Polly headed to Pete.

Pete put it in the net!

The game was fast and furious! Belmont School had one goal, but soon Greenhill had two!

Belmont
Pass it to Polly!
Come on Greenhill!
Polly!
Belmont School for ever!
Run, Nisha!
Up Belmont!
TESCO

But a big boy from Greenhill was out to get Polly.

He raced up behind her and stuck out his foot – a dirty trick!

Polly jumped!

She swerved!

She kicked the ball right between the posts!

Just as the final whistle blew.

The match was a draw!

Mr Budd asked Mr Patel to help coach the football team.

MORE BOOKS BY SARAH GARLAND FROM FRANCES LINCOLN CHILDREN'S BOOKS

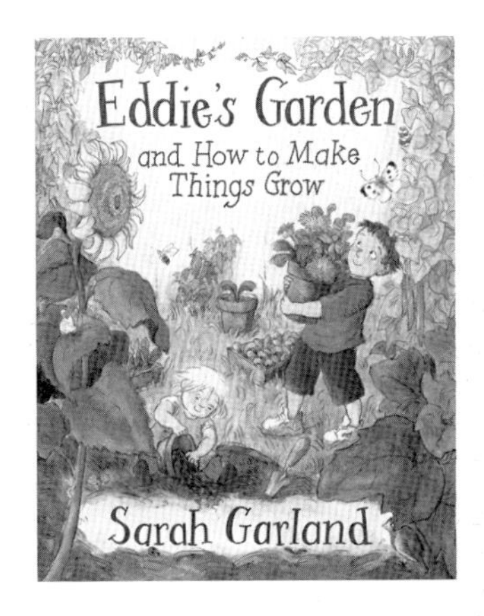

Eddie's Garden and How to Make Things Grow

What makes Eddie's Garden grow?
Earth, rain, warm sun, and all sorts of creatures!
Eddie works hard in his garden – digging, pulling up the weeds and watering his plants. Soon the garden looks wonderful, full of tasty treats that will make his picnic with Lily, Mum and Grandad the best one ever!

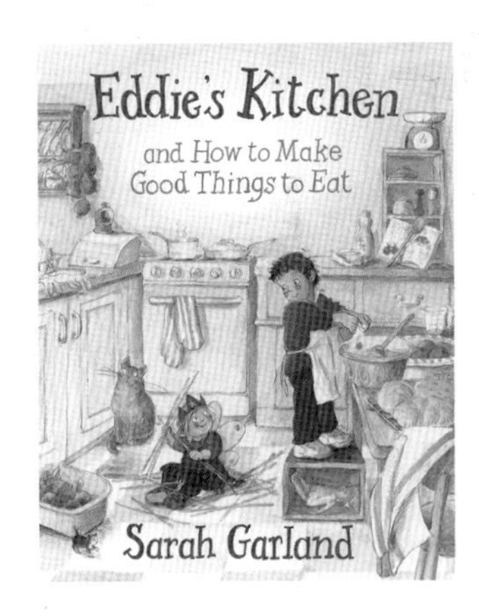

Eddie's Kitchen and How to Make Good Things to Eat

It is Grandad's birthday so Eddie and Mum are making a birthday feast – with Lily's help, of course!
Crusty bread and spaghetti, eggs from their chickens, a delicious orange cake – soon the table is filled with scrumptious birthday treats. But what has Lily done with all the carrots?

Billy and Belle

Billy and Belle can't wait for Mum to have the new baby!
When the special day arrives, Dad takes Mum to hospital while Belle is allowed to spend the day with Billy at school. It's pet day, so Billy's hamster comes too. Everything goes to plan – until Belle gets into a spot of trouble over a pet spider!